D0993805

Dead Cooler

Written and illustrated

by

Peter Clover

You do not need to read this page – just get on with the book!

First published in 2007 in Great Britain by
Barrington Stoke Ltd
18 Walker St, Edinburgh, EH3 7LP

www.barringtonstoke.co.uk

ISBN: 978-1-84299-387-3

Printed in Great Britain by Bell & Bain Ltd

AUTHOR AND ILLUSTRATOR ID

Name: Peter Clover

Likes: Sunshine, hugs
and Pot Noodles

Dislikes: Grey rainy days,
lumpy porridge and bullies

3 words that best describe me:
Comical. Crazy. Caring.

A secret that not many people know:
I am an alien from the planet Gal'Axor

For Gary and Mandy

Contents

The First Bit

Sammy Blue was just like any other normal kid. It was his new friends – Smitty and the gang – who were totally different.

Smitty and the gang were pirates. Real, live pirates. Well, they weren't exactly 'live' any more. In fact they were all dead. You see, Smitty and the gang were ghosts. Sammy's new friends were crew members of the Black Crow, a pirate ship which had sunk over 250 years ago.

Smitty was the cabin boy. Then there was Bacon – the ship's cook. And Doc Bones and Squire Delaney. There was Boris the Bosun, and seven sulky deck hands. Oh, and there were also two whacking great cats and a dusty old parrot called Captain Crabmeat.

Smitty and the gang lived in Sammy's tiny bedroom, in a small flat, high above Mr Hackbone's bric-a-brac antique shop.

No one except Sammy and his own parrot, Polly, could see the pirate ghosts. That was really cool – Dead Cool!

Chapter 1
Pirate Parties

Sammy sat in bed. He was reading his footie mags before he went to sleep.

The tiny bedroom smelled strongly of salty sand, seaweed and fishy herrings. Sammy smiled as he listened to the creaks and groans of the old ship's timbers. His bed rocked gently to and fro. A ship's lantern swung from an oak beam above his head and its golden light lit the rough cabin walls. It was just as if Sammy was on board the Black Crow itself, and the ship was swaying and bobbing on the Seven Seas.

Sammy's bedroom had been like that ever since Smitty and the pirates had moved in. The room looked normal to everyone else. But for Sammy, it was always a ship's cabin. Even the bedroom window had changed into a ship's port-hole with brass all round it. But no one else could see that.

A swirling mist crept slowly across the floor. Thin trails of silver smoke rose up and twisted into a shape Sammy knew well. It was Smitty, the cabin boy.

Smitty was about the same age as Sammy, but pale grey in colour from head to toe. And Sammy could see right through him. He was dressed in shabby trousers cut off at the knee, and a tatty cotton shirt. His hair was long, matted, and tied back at the neck in a rat's tail.

"Ahoy, shipmate," bellowed Smitty with a cheeky grin. His dark eyes sparkled.

"Strike up the Jolly Roger," screeched Crabmeat from the cage in the corner. He squawked so loudly and so suddenly that Polly woke with a fright and fell off her perch with a thump.

"Where have you been all day?" Sammy wanted to know. He looked at his bedside clock. It was half past nine. "And where are the others?"

Before Smitty had time to answer, the other eleven members of the Black Crow fell through the walls and staggered into the room.

They were very noisy and singing loudly. "Yo ho ho and a bottle of rum, we kicked Captain Redbeard's bum," they roared.

"You're drunk!" said Sammy.

"We've been having a party," grinned Squire Delaney. "Hic!"

"But you had a party yesterday," said Sammy. "And the day before that. *And* the day before that as well!"

"We're pirates," said Doc Bones. "Pirates have parties. Hic! And now that we've stopped running away from Redbeard the Really Rotten, we get a bit bored. We've got nothing to do!"

"If only we could come to school, like you said," added Smitty with a cheeky grin.

"Yes. Please let us come to school," Doc Bones begged.

"Pretty P-L-E-A-S-E?" asked Boris the Bosun.

"Please, please, give us a squeeze," squawked Crabmeat, with a flutter of dusty feathers.

Suddenly, Smitty and all the pirates jumped onto Sammy's bed and covered him with boozy pirate kisses.

"Please let us come to school, Sammy. Please. Please. Please!"

Chapter 2
Off to School

The next morning, Sammy woke bright and early.

"Rise and shine, you miserable lot," he chirped loudly. Then he jumped out of bed and pulled back the curtains. Bright sunshine flooded into the cabin.

"Aargghh!" cried Squire Delaney and put his hand over his eyes. "Are we being attacked?"

"Prepare the cannons!" yelled Boris the Bosun.

"What time is it?" moaned Smitty. His voice came from inside the mattress.

"Eight o'clock," said Sammy. "And school starts at nine, so get your skates on."

"I haven't got any skates," said Doc Bones. "And can't I stay here? My head hurts!"

"No, you can't," Sammy said firmly. "Last night you all wanted to go to school. So today, YOU'RE GOING! Now, move it!"

****

Seacliff Primary was a broken-down sort of school. With old, messy classrooms. The walls had carved wood panels all round them. There were desks, not tables. And all the desks had round holes in their lids to put ink pots in, like in schools long ago.

Sammy's desk was right at the back of the classroom. It sat in a cosy corner next to a big, round window which was just like a ship's port-hole. It was the only round window in the old, crumbling, run-down school.

Sammy thought it was the best desk ever. He could see everyone in the classroom and he didn't even have to turn around.

He could also peer out through the window, across the rooftops, and down on to the old fishing harbour of Seacliff. Beyond the harbour, Sammy could see a wide stretch of sparkling blue sea. That was brilliant. It was definitely the best desk in the whole wide world.

The only bad thing about Sammy's desk was that it was right smack bang next to Nosey Josey's.

Nosey Josey was the classroom creep. She was a sneaky, trouble-making snitch. She was always running to the teachers and telling tales. No one liked her.

Sammy sat at his desk and waited as the other children settled down into their seats. He hid his rucksack under the desk. Smitty came and plonked himself down next to Sammy. They watched the classroom fill up. The rest of the pirate crew were fast asleep inside Sammy's rucksack. Because they were ghosts, they never took up any space.

Crabmeat, the phantom parrot, had somehow got himself stuck inside Sammy's desk. He poked his dusty head up through the ink pot hole and began squawking at the top of his voice.

"Ahoy there, me shipmates! Splice the mainbrace! Weigh the anchor! Pieces of eight! Pieces of eight!"

Sammy squashed his hand over the hole as fast as he could. He had to stop the parrot's noise. Then he remembered – he was the only one who could see or hear the ghostly pirates or their pet bird.

That's why it was really odd when Nosey Josey suddenly looked over and said in a very loud voice, "What was that? It sounded just like a parrot!"

Chapter 3
A Pirate Portrait

Miss Brownweed came into the classroom. She was Sammy's teacher. She stood behind her desk at the front.

"Good morning, Class Four," she said.

"Good morning, Miss Brownweed," the class answered.

"Brownweed, Brownseed," screeched Crabmeat from inside Sammy's desk.

Nosey Josey looked around the room again with a puzzled look on her face. She glared right at Sammy.

Sammy stuffed some paper into the ink pot hole in his desk.

Miss Brownweed looked round the class, smiled and started to talk to them all.

"Today," she said, "we're going to learn all about pirates."

Eleven pirate heads suddenly poked out of Sammy's rucksack. Then eleven pairs of sleepy eyes suddenly opened wide, as Miss Brownweed took an enormous painting out of an enormous cardboard package that was propped up by her desk.

"You may or may not know," began Miss Brownweed. "But before this was a school, it was the home of one Horatio Hornblaster –

a famous and terrible pirate who vanished without a trace, in the year 1706."

"Horrible Horatio Hornblaster," Smitty hissed. "We've heard of him, haven't we, lads? The most horrible pirate that ever lived!"

"Horatio Hornblaster?" said Squire Delaney. "No. No. No. He wasn't HORRIBLE at all. He was a gentleman. There wasn't a nicer pirate that sailed the Seven Seas."

"Nice, nice, nice," agreed Doc Bones. "Always said please and thank you when he robbed anyone."

Sammy pushed the rucksack further under the desk with his foot. The pirate crew were getting a bit loud. And Nosey Josey was staring at Sammy's bag with her mouth hanging open like a trap door.

"The Town Hall has said we can borrow this wonderful painting of Horatio Hornblaster," Miss Brownweed went on. "I was told it used to hang in this very room," she said. "That was when this was a house, not Seacliff Primary." Miss Brownweed turned the painting around to show it to the class. It was an elegant portrait of an elegant pirate in a very elegant gold-edged picture frame.

Smitty gasped and fell off the chair. The painting was so life-like. "That's Horrible Horatio Hornblaster alright," he muttered under his breath.

Horatio Hornblaster wore a fine blue velvet coat, with shining buttons, tassels and loops of silver ribbon. A fancy lace collar was tied round his scrawny neck. Glossy golden locks tumbled over his narrow shoulders. And a thin, elegant moustache was waxed and curled into two

wicked spikes at the corners of his mean mouth. It was Horrible Horatio Hornblaster in all his best clothes! A perfect pirate portrait. A pirate masterpiece!

Behind the painted pirate sailed his pirate galleon – the Laughing Looney. Its black sails were billowing, its cannons blazing.

"Isn't he something to see?" smiled Miss Brownweed, looking impressed. "Horatio Hornblaster is perhaps the most famous pirate of all time. And he lived right here, in the house he built, before it became our school."

The classroom was filled with the cooing sounds of "Oooo"s and "Ahhh"s.

"Please, Miss," cut in Nosey Josey. "My father says that ALL pirates are smelly, nasty, toe rags!"

Smitty was shocked. How could anyone say that? Some of his nicest friends were pirates! Smitty was a pirate! He took a deep breath, blew hard and sent Nosey Josey's books and paper fluttering off her desk. He also filled the classroom with the smell of rotten fish.

Josey bent down to pick up all her things. Miss Brownweed fanned her nose and glanced at Josey's bum.

"It's a bit hot and stuffy in here," she said. "Open your window a bit more, Sammy. We need some air in here."

The class sniggered as Sammy pushed the window wide open. Outside the morning sunlight danced across the harbour below. Then Sammy noticed a blurred shape on the water far away.

It was hardly more than a skeleton of broken masts and ragged rigging. But the ghostly shape of a pirate galleon was appearing.

Sammy looked back to the portrait of Horatio Hornblaster. The pirate seemed to be looking right back at him, with an evil grin.

Chapter 4
Pirate Treasure

On one of the wooden panels in the classroom, there was a carving of a laughing seagull. Miss Brownweed hung the pirate portrait on its grinning beak. Then she began to talk to the class again.

"There have been many stories told about Horatio Hornblaster and his ship, the Laughing Looney," she began. "Some people think he was the nastiest pirate that ever sailed. But others say that he was a Robin Hood of the seas. That he robbed only the richest merchant ships so as to bring food and clothes to the poor people of Seacliff."

Smitty shifted in his seat and looked back up at the portrait.

"No one knows for sure," the teacher went on. "But what we do know is that one moonlit night, as Hornblaster's ship lay moored in the harbour, a terrible storm sprang up. The wild waves drove the ship against a reef of ragged rocks beyond the bay. The Laughing Looney, and Horatio Hornblaster, vanished without a trace."

"My father says it was good riddance to bad rubbish," Nosey Josey blurted out. "He says that ALL pirates are no more than common crooks."

This was too much for Smitty. He wasn't having that! Before Sammy could do anything to stop him, Smitty had lifted the waste-paper bin and emptied it over Nosey Josey's head.

Everyone was looking at the fine portrait of Horatio Hornblaster, so no one saw it happen. All they heard was Josie's muffled shouts. And, when they turned to look, all they saw was Nosey Josey covered in rubbish, with an old banana skin squashed on top of her head, and a pencil stuck up her nose.

"What on earth are you doing, Josey?" snapped Miss Brownweed. "Sit down at once. Stop messing around."

"But the bin just jumped up and emptied itself over me," bleated Josey. "I didn't do anything. I didn't touch it, I swear!"

"Don't be so silly," said Miss Brownweed with a scowl. "Now sit down. Or go outside!"

Nosey Josey sat down.

Miss Brownweed went on with the lesson.

"Today," she announced, "is Friday 13th, and it's exactly 300 years since Horatio Hornblaster and his ship vanished from Seacliff."

Smitty settled himself back down as Miss Brownweed went on.

"The missing treasure ..." she started to say.

"TREASURE!" Smitty jumped up again. He was so excited that for a few seconds, he drained all the electricity from the light bulbs. The computer screen on Miss

Brownweed's desk flickered. And Sammy's rucksack rolled out from under his desk like a remote-controlled bowling ball.

"The missing treasure," Miss Brwonweed told them, "was *never* found. Some people say that there never *was* any treasure. While others think," whispered Miss Brownweed, "that the treasure is hidden right here, somewhere in this very school building!"

"Has anyone ever hunted for the treasure in the school, Miss?" someone asked.

Before anyone could answer Nosey Josey butted in. "It's all just a load of rubbish! My father says if there *was* any pirate treasure, then it would have been found years ago."

"Perhaps he's right," Miss Brownweed said with a smile. "Many times, over the years, people have looked for the treasure in the school. But no one has ever found even a tiny clue to tell them where the treasure could be hidden!" The teacher turned to face the pirate portrait. "And so," she said, "everyone just gave up, and stopped looking."

"I bet WE could find it," Smitty said loudly. "I bet WE could find Horrible Hornblaster's secret treasure!" And with that, he shot up off the seat and floated happily through the ceiling.

The rest of the pirate gang floated up after him. They burst out of Sammy's rucksack like supersonic rockets and zoomed up behind Smitty.

Sammy shivered as the classroom suddenly turned icy cold. A green mist swirled across the floor. And the wooden panels on the walls began to creak and groan like a ship's hull. The smell of fishy herrings filled the room.

"What's that stink?" Nosey Josey said and screwed up her nose. "This is something to do with you, Sammy. Isn't it? Something fishy's going on!"

No one else could smell a thing. Or see the eleven pairs of legs dangling through the ceiling above their heads. The pirate crew were half in the room, and half through the ceiling. Their heads were up in the empty attic space above the classroom as they looked up there for Hornblaster's treasure.

Nosey Josey looked up, suddenly. *She* saw everything. Then she fell back off her seat. And fainted.

Chapter 5
Stepping Out

When Josey woke up, she was lying on the classroom floor. Twelve pirate faces were grinning down at her, through the ceiling.

Sammy looked up at the gang, and scowled.

Pop! Pop! Pop! The pirate faces vanished back into the ceiling.

"Josey! I won't tell you again," boomed Miss Brownweed.

"But, Miss ..."

"If you bother us once more, you will have to leave the classroom." The teacher fixed Josey with an icy look.

Nosey Josey turned back to Sammy and gave him a mean look.

"Now pay attention, everyone." Miss Brownweed held up a DVD. "I've got a short film here," she said. "It's all about the most famous pirates in history." She popped the disc into the computer.

The film started.

On the computer screen was a big picture of a fantastic treasure chest. Rich jewels and gold spilled out. At once twelve pirate faces popped back through the ceiling.

"Shiver me timbers. There it is," yelled Smitty. "There's the treasure, lads! We've found it. Right there! We've found Horrible Hornblaster's missing treasure."

The pirate gang all streamed from the ceiling in a swirling green whoosh, and vanished, with a mighty *ZAP*, into the computer screen.

Sammy tried not to look. Smitty and the pirate gang were now *in* the computer screen, with the treasure chest.

"We've found the treasure," shouted Doc Bones. "But how do we get it out of this funny box?"

The computer flashed and whirred. The class watched the computer screen as

Squire Delaney and three deck hands tried hard to lift the pirate chest.

"I don't remember this part of the film," said Miss Brownweed.

Next Smitty's face showed up, with his nose squashed against the computer screen – from the inside!

"Help us, Sammy. We're trapped," mouthed Smitty. "Get us out of here."

"I think there must be something wrong with the computer," said the teacher. Thick, green smoke began to pour from the back of the monitor.

Sammy jumped up and quickly ejected the DVD. Smitty and the gang were hurled back into the classroom with a huge force of electric energy. And then something really *incredible* happened.

Sammy couldn't believe it. Nosey Josey didn't want to look. Instead, she pulled her school bag over her head, as Horrible Horatio Hornblaster stepped out of his portrait into the classroom.

Chapter 6
Pirate in the Playground

"Ahoy there, me hearties," roared Horatio Hornblaster. "I've been waiting 300 years to stretch these stiff, painted legs!"

Somehow, the pirate in the painting had suddenly come to life. He stood in the middle of the classroom waving a cutlass above his head.

Miss Brownweed was trying to re-boot the computer. Sammy and Josey were the only ones who could see Horatio Hornblaster.

Nosey Josey still had her school bag over her head. She peeped out and whimpered softly.

"Arrrr! Get me to my ship," bellowed Hornblaster. "I set sail today!"

Sammy peered out through the window at the harbour below.

He could just make out the Laughing Looney in Seacliff Harbour. The ship was getting bigger and more real all the time. Under Hornblaster's spell, its broken timbers were growing strong and sturdy. Huge black sails billowed from the masts, waiting to sail with Hornblaster again, across the Seven Seas.

Sammy put his head in his hands. He'd had no idea that bringing Smitty and the gang to school would ever turn into THIS!

Suddenly, the dinner bell rang. *Brriiinnngggg!*

Sammy almost jumped out of his skin with fright.

"We'll carry on with this after lunch," smiled Miss Brownweed.

As everyone picked up their lunch-boxes and pushed out of the classroom, Smitty and the pirates stood and stared at the empty pirate portrait hanging on the wall.

When Horatio Hornblaster stepped out of his painting, he'd dropped something from his pocket and left it behind on the painted grass.

Outside in the playground, Sammy opened his lunchbox. Nosey Josey was spying on him from behind the bike sheds, watching everything he did.

Sammy was just about to take a bite out of his tuna fish and strawberry jam sandwich when Horrible Horatio Hornblaster suddenly appeared behind him.

Swipe! The pirate's cutlass speared the sandwich and flipped it out of Sammy's hand.

Nosey Josey watched in amazement. Sammy's sandwich was slowly vanishing into thin air, bite by bite.

"Mmm, that was deliciously nasty," said Hornblaster, and he wiped his mouth on his lace sleeve. "The first grub I've had for 300 years."

Hornblaster placed his ghostly hand on Sammy's arm.

"Now I want YOU," he said, "to row me to my ship."

Sammy suddenly felt very odd. His head began to spin. He felt dizzy. As Hornblaster led him out of the school gates, Sammy felt as if he was walking in a dream.

The sky was getting darker and darker as if a storm was on the way. Seacliff Harbour began to glow with a green haze, as the Laughing Looney sailed into full view.

To everyone else, the day was bright and sunny. To Sammy, it was night – dark and moonlit with a storm coming.

"300 years ago to this very day," said Hornblaster, "my ship and I were lost to a storm. Now we are both here again. And it's up to YOU, Sammy lad, to bring us both together!"

Sammy followed Hornblaster down towards the moonlit harbour below. The phantom pirate held his cutlass in front of him and pointed the way.

A little way behind, a sneaky shadow followed them. It was Nosey Josey.

"So! Maybe there is a secret treasure after all," she muttered to herself. "And Sammy Blue is being shown the way." Her eyes shone with greed. "Well, if there IS pirate gold up for grabs, then I'm having some of it!" As quick as a flash, she dived down a dark alleyway. She knew a good short cut to get to the harbour before Sammy and Hornblaster. There she would find a place to hide.

Chapter 7
A Secret Stowaway

The time had come. Under Hornblaster's spell, darkness settled on Seacliff Harbour. Hornblaster was ready to join his ship once more.

A haunting wind filled the Laughing Looney's black sails. From the harbour, Horatio Hornblaster waved his cutlass to his ghostly crew. They cheered back at him from the ghostly galleon.

"Arrrr! Sammy, lad," said Hornblaster
with a grin. "Everyone knows that a pirate
captain must *never, ever,* row himself out
to his own ship. It's very bad luck. So *you*
must do the honour and row for me!"

Sammy didn't trust Hornblaster. But
what could he do? The pirate's spell was too
strong. Sammy clambered into a wooden
row boat that was tied at the harbour wall,

slowly lifted the oars, and began to row towards the ghostly galleon.

It wasn't long before the row boat hit the Laughing Looney's great wooden hull. It bumped into the ship with a dull thunk. A sudden wave spat salty spray into Sammy's face. And in that instant, Sammy woke up and shook off Hornblaster's spell. Above his head, a wooden chair was being let down by Horrible Hornblaster's ghostly crew. The wooden seat dangled from rusty chains like a garden swing.

"It's been a long time since I've been swung aboard," whispered Hornblaster. He glanced at Sammy. "I've actually forgotten how to do it," he said. "I think *you* should try it out first. It would be *terrible*, if after waiting 300 years for this moment, something tragic happened to me!"

Sammy looked up at the vast creaking hull. He could see the ship's painted figurehead – a mean-looking, laughing bird with great wings spread back against the wooden bows.

Sammy was wide awake now. *If he got on board the ship, would he ever get off?* he thought to himself.

"If you can get up on board ship in that chair," hissed Hornblaster, "there will be a rich reward. Pirate gold. As much as you can carry!"

Sammy swayed to and fro as he stood up. His legs shook. He really did not want to climb into that chair and board the ghostly galleon.

Where are you, Smitty? he thought. *What should I do?*

Sammy's thoughts hung in the cold air. Suddenly Smitty's cheeky face appeared in a rolling wave. The wave turned into the shape of an enormous hand which smacked the little row boat. It rocked wildly and Sammy fell flat on his back.

Then suddenly, the pile of old fishing nets stuffed at the back of the row boat flew up into the air. Nosey Josey jumped out of her hiding place.

"I'll do it, Mr Hornblaster, sir. I'll show you how to ride the stupid chair," Josey screeched.

The ghostly roar of laughing pirates filled the air as Nosey Josey jumped into the wooden seat and was hauled up into the darkness on swinging chains.

"Arrrr! That's the way to get aboard, ain't it!" shrieked Hornblaster. "And that's the way to trick a greedy new prisoner. Works every time!"

Horrible Horatio Hornblaster sprang up as the chair dropped down again. This time, he jumped into it easily, kicked out his legs, and flew up into the air.

Suddenly, up out of the water rose a figure. It was Smitty.

"What about Josie?" gasped Sammy.

"Don't worry about HER," said Smitty, "Hornblaster won't be able to keep her for long. Just ROW!"

Sammy picked up the oars and rowed as fast as he could back to the harbour. Only when he was safely back on dry land did he dare look back. The afternoon sun was already starting to shine again as the Laughing Looney sailed out of the bay. Sammy looked at Smitty and shivered, as the pirate galleon faded, then vanished into thin air.

Chapter 8
A Pirate's Riddle

Sammy walked back into the classroom just as the afternoon bell stopped ringing.

Everyone was sitting at their desks. Everyone except Nosey Josey!

Miss Brownweed was looking hard at Horatio Hornblaster's portrait. No one else but Sammy could see that the pirate had gone. All Sammy could see in the painting was green grass, rocks and blue sky.

"I'm sorry to say that the computer's crashed," said Miss Brownweed. "So, instead of watching the DVD, I'd like you all to make up a story in your writing books about where in the school you think Horatio Hornblaster might have hidden his secret treasure."

"I'd hide it up the chimney, Miss," said Steven, a boy at the front of the class.

"Very good," smiled Miss Brownweed. "But I think that's one of the first places that people would have looked."

"I'd hide it in my desk, Miss," said a girl.

"I'd hide it in the bogs, Miss," shouted another boy.

Miss Brownweed smiled at all the crazy ideas.

"Don't shout out! Save it all for your stories," she said. "Now, one by one, I want you to come and take a good look at the painting before you begin. Starting at the back with Sammy Blue."

Sammy walked up to the front and looked up at the empty portrait. Where had Smitty got to? Then he peered into the picture and saw Smitty there, with the rest of the gang, behind some rocks. They were all looking hard at something in Smitty's hand.

Crabmeat, the parrot, was perched on top of the gold frame.

"Treasure's about. Treasure's about," he squawked, loudly.

Smitty looked up, then hurried to the front of the painting.

"We've found some kind of map," he babbled. "But we can't work it out." He handed the map out of the painting to Sammy. "It's written in a funny way," Smitty said. "Can you read it?"

"Don't take too long, Sammy," said Miss Brownweed. "There are others waiting!"

Sammy hurried back to his desk. Smitty floated along behind him.

He looked at the map Smitty had given him. This was not a normal treasure map written on paper or pirate parchment. This was a lace handkerchief!

Sammy grinned. Horatio Hornblaster's fancy lace hanky had been used as a blotter, to blot the ink when Hornblaster wrote his treasure map. The writing on the pirate's hanky was an imprint. That's why it was all back to front.

Sammy put the handkerchief, *the wrong way round*, flat against the window. Bright sunlight shone through it. Now Sammy could read the writing easily.

"It's a riddle," said Sammy.

"Riddles. Tiddles. Cats do piddles," squawked Crabmeat.

This is what Sammy read:

In the Harbour Room with a port-hole view,

Stand in a ring that is golden for you.

Look to the ceiling. Look to the floor.

Search for the Looney.

There's treasure galore.

It was a very odd riddle. But Sammy was good at puzzles. He thought about the words for a moment, then gazed out of the window at the harbour below.

*In the Harbour Room with a port-hole
view.*

"That's it," said Sammy. "It's got to be
this room. This is the only round window in
the school. And you can see the harbour
down below."

The riddle was beginning to make sense.

*Stand in a ring that is golden for
you.*

The sunlight was shining through the
round window and made a bright circle of
light on the wooden floorboards. Sammy
felt very excited now. He got up and went
to stand inside the golden ring.

Now what? Sammy didn't know what to
do next.

Look to the ceiling. Look to the floor.

What was he looking for?

"*Search for the Looney, there's treasure galore*. That's what the riddle said." Sammy turned to Smitty. "The Looney. That's the name of Hornblaster's ship, isn't it?"

"Aye," said Smitty. "But a LOON ... that's also the name of a sea-bird."

Suddenly, Sammy remembered seeing the painted figurehead of a laughing bird on the hull of Hornblaster's galleon.

"That's it," exclaimed Sammy. "The Laughing Looney is a sea-bird. Hornblaster's treasure is hidden in this very room. And the key to it is a laughing bird!"

Sammy scanned the room from floor to ceiling. He looked at the wooden wall panels. All kinds of birds and animals were carved into the polished wood. One by one Sammy checked them over. And at last he found what he was looking for! Hornblaster's pirate portrait was hanging from the grinning beak of a laughing bird.

"Miss! Miss! I think I know where the treasure is hidden!" yelled Sammy.

"Oh, yes. Very good," smiled the teacher. "And I hope you've written it all down in your story."

"She doesn't believe you," whispered Smitty.

"The treasure's hidden in this classroom, Miss." Sammy tried again.

Miss Brownweed clapped her hands together. "That sounds excellent, Sammy," she chirped. "I can't wait to read what you've written."

It was no good! Miss Brownweed just wasn't listening!

"There's only one thing to do," said Smitty. "Come on lads, it's treasure time!"

All the pirates answered the call. They streamed out of the painting, and crowded around the carving of the laughing looney.

"Try pushing it," said Sammy.

"Pardon!" said Miss Brownweed.

"Give it a twist!" Sammy added.

"Are you feeling alright, Sammy?" Miss Brownweed was looking at him in a worried way.

"Maybe it needs pulling?" Sammy added.

"*Heave ho, me hearties!*" sang Smitty.

"Give it a yank!"

The pirate gang heaved and pushed at the carving. They pulled it and shoved it. They twisted it and turned it. But nothing happened. The laughing looney didn't move.

Smitty and the gang looked fed up. They slowly floated back down to the floor. "We can't do it," grumbled Doc Bones.

"Bother!" said Sammy.

"Are you feeling unwell?" asked the teacher.

Suddenly, there was a flapping of dusty wings as Crabmeat flew up to the carved sea-bird.

"Who are *you* laughing at?" squawked the parrot. Then he gave the looney a really sharp tap on the head with his heavy beak.

Suddenly, the classroom was filled with the groaning sound of creaking wood, like ship's timbers moving with the sea. Everyone fell silent as the old wooden wall panels slowly began to slide apart.

"*Treasure!*" yelled Smitty. "We've found Hornblaster's hidden treasure!"

With an enormous whoosh, more gold coins than Sammy could ever have dreamed of spilled into the room. Thousands of gold doubloons poured out from behind the walls. It was like winning the jackpot on a slot machine in a casino.

Diamonds, rubies and emeralds sparkled like Christmas fairy lights behind the wooden panels. The walls were stuffed with pirate treasure.

"Oh, Sammy. You clever boy," praised Miss Brownweed. "I don't know how you did it, but this has turned out to be the best pirate lesson EVER!"

Smitty and the crew were dancing in a big circle, singing and whooping with laughter.

"Going to school is better than any pirate party," yelled Squire Delaney.

"We've never had so much fun," agreed Boris the Bosun.

"Can we come again tomorrow?" asked Bacon, the ship's cook.

Sammy was about to tell them that school wasn't always this exciting. But they were having so much fun, he decided to say nothing. Today had been really cool. Dead Cool!

The End Bit

In case you want to know what happened to Hornblaster's treasure – the money was all used to turn the old school back into a house again. But this time it became a pirate museum in honour of the famous, the horrible, Horatio Hornblaster – the richest pirate who ever lived. A brand new school was built next door with the rest of the money.

Oh ... and I almost forgot! Just like Smitty said, Nosey Josey turned up later that same afternoon. She was down by the harbour. She had seaweed in her hair. And a jellyfish down the back of her knickers. But she couldn't remember a thing that had happened. And she couldn't see pirate ghosts any more. Which for Sammy and Smitty was Dead Cool – in fact, *Dead Cooler!*

Barrington Stoke would like to thank all its readers for commenting on the manuscript before publication and in particular:

Brian O'Neill
Tom Fewlass
Nick Rees
George Chunilal
Sebastian Koenig
Ben Barclay
Conrad Getty
J Carter-Brown

Become a Consultant!

Would you like to give us feedback on our titles before they are published? Contact us at the email address below – we'd love to hear from you!

info@barringtonstoke.co.uk
www.barringtonstoke.co.uk